For Larsson and Talan,
our newest little superheroes

The art for this book was created by engraving on an ink-coated clay board. Color was added using a wireless drawing tablet and a variety of Adobe software to create the final art. The drawing tablet can always be used again!

The text was set in CCComicrazy, and the display type is BlambotCasual and LCD. The book title was created by David Coulson. This book was printed on Chinese Senbrand 100% recycled matte art paper.

• Little, Brown and Company • Hachette Book Group • 1290 Avenue of the Americas, New York, NY 10104 • Visit us at lb-kids.com • Little, Brown and Company is a division of Hachette Book Group, Inc. The Little, Brown name and logo are trademarks of Hachette Book Group, Inc. • The publisher is not responsible for websites (or their content) that are not owned by the publisher. • First Edition: March 2013 • Library of Congress Cataloging-in-Publication Data • Gall, Chris. • Awesome Dawson / Chris Gall. — 1st ed. • p. cm. • Summary: All his life, Dawson has been inventing things, repairing toys in unusual ways, and helping clean up his neighborhood by reusing discarded objects, but when his Vacu-Maniac malfunctions it is his friend Mooey whose brainpower saves the day. — ISBN 978-0-316-21330-1 • [1. Inventors—Fiction. 2. Recycling (Waste)— Fiction. 3. Toys—Fiction. 4. Imagination—Fiction. 5. Humorous stories.] I. Title. • PZ7.G1352Awe 2013 [E]—dc23 • 2012026496 • 10 9 8 7 6 5 4 3 • APS • PRINTED IN CHINA • Book design by Tracy Shaw

When I was a baby,
I invented a new kind of hat.

Later, I made a space helmet,

a motorboat,

and a fun way to get to school.

Today I'm trying out some new bodies for Mooey. I like to experiment!

I really need to find a way to get my chores done so I can work on Mooey. There must be something here I can use to help me. . . .

I pull out a broken rake, a broom, and a watering can. Then I find a gum-ball machine and a pool hose.

This will be my best invention ever!

I give it my list of chores to do.

This Vacu-Maniac sure is powerful. It's sucking up everything in my workshop!

Uh-oh. The Vacu-Maniac is getting bigger with everything it eats!

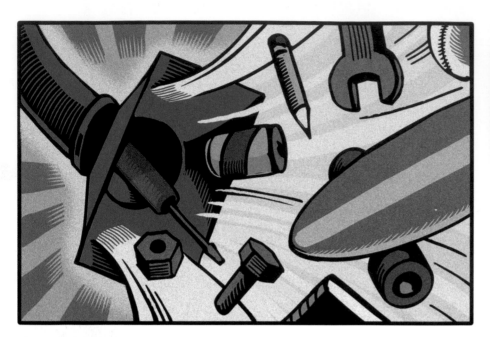

We need to do something! Mooey and I jump into my airplane. Up here we can see the Vacu-Maniac's path of destruction. There go our trees and my swing set . . . and Dad's car! The Maniac is growing bigger by the minute!

I look around for things I can use. EVERYTHING can be used again.

CLANK. The Vacu-Maniac is slowing down. Mooey is putting it to sleep!

Then Mooey opens the front hatch, and everything inside comes pouring out—including me!

But I still find a way to make my chores a little easier.

Plus, Mom and Dad really deserve a new car!
SURPRISE!
UMBRELLA
AIRPLANE RUDDER
JET ENGINE
HOT TUB
HOT ROD ENGINE
MONSTER TRUCK
SPEEDBOAT

And I didn't forget about Mooey, either.

10/08

...crackers

spring
couplets

decorated
kumquat tree

broom

whole fish

gong

spring
lantern

THIS IS A BORZOI BOOK PUBLISHED BY ALFRED A. KNOPF

Copyright © 2008 by Grace Lin
All rights reserved.
Published in the United States by Alfred A. Knopf, an imprint of Random House
Children's Books, a division of Random House, Inc., New York.

KNOPF, BORZOI BOOKS, and the colophon are registered trademarks of Random House, Inc.
www.randomhouse.com/kids
Educators and librarians, for a variety of teaching tools, visit us at
www.randomhouse.com/teachers
Library of Congress Cataloging-in-Publication Data
[CIP Information]

The illustrations in this book were created using Turner Design Gouache
on Arches hot-press paper.

MANUFACTURED IN CHINA

JANUARY 2008

10 9 8 7 6 5 4 3 2 1

First Edition

To my niece Lily,
who I hope continues to bring
in every New Year smiling

Bringing In the NEW YEAR

新年快樂

Grace Lin

ALFRED A. KNOPF
NEW YORK

Is the New Year coming?
I hope so!
We try to welcome it in.

So, Jie-Jie
sweeps the old
year out of the house.

Ba-Ba hangs the spring-happiness poems.

Ma-Ma makes the get-rich dumplings.

Mei-Mei gets a fresh haircut.

And I put on my new *qi pao*
dress for the New Year feast.
Now will the New Year come?

Pop! Pop! Pop!
Do you hear the firecrackers?
Are they bringing in the New Year?

No! But they brought in the lions. They're here to scare away last year's bad luck.

They scare Mei-Mei too.
Don't cry, Mei-Mei!

Where is the New Year?
We carry the lanterns to light its way.

I hope the New Year
follows us soon.

Look, there's the dragon!
Auntie is waking him up by opening his eyes.
The New Year must be coming.

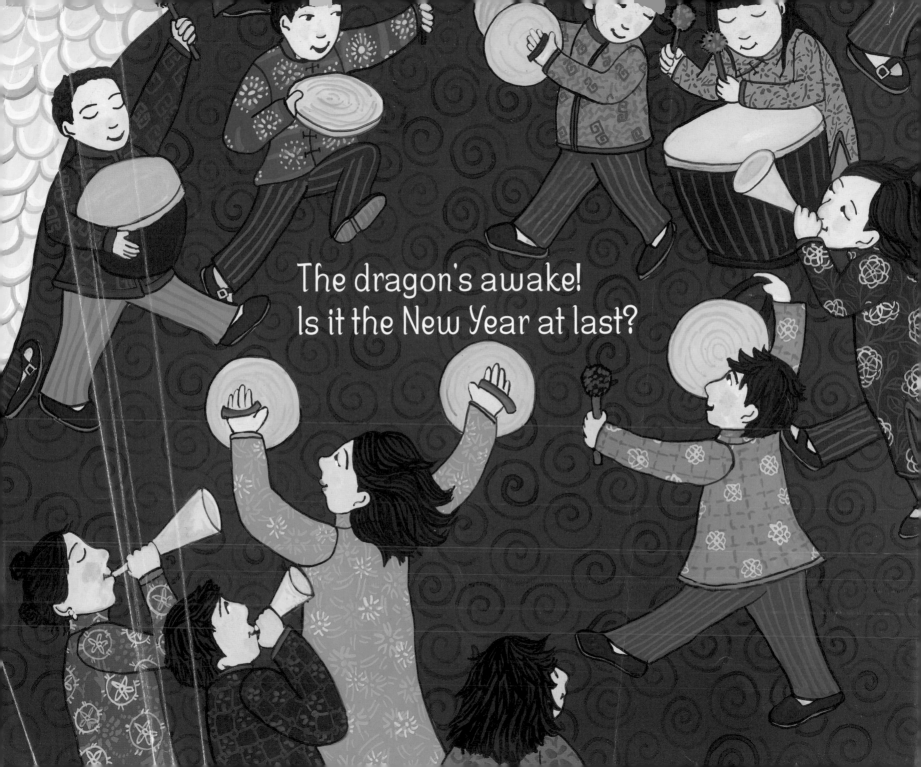

The dragon's awake!
Is it the New Year at last?

Yes, hooray!
The New Year is here!
Happy New Year,
everyone!

Chinese New Year, which is now more commonly called Lunar New Year (since it is based on the lunar calendar and many other countries besides China observe it), is one of the most celebrated holidays in the world. It is such an important festival that it traditionally lasted for fifteen days, ending with the Lantern Festival. Nowadays, however, most people just celebrate for one day. It is a time for families and friends to get together and is the biggest, most exciting event of the year.

There are many customs and traditions associated with the New Year. People prepare for this festival for almost a month ahead of time. Houses are cleaned (to sweep away the old year), debts are paid (so the New Year begins without obligation), and red decorations featuring spring poems and good wishes are put up to welcome in the New Year (red is considered a lucky color). People also prepare themselves—cutting their hair and buying new clothes. All this is done so the New Year can start fresh.

To make sure that the New Year is full of plenty of food and luck, people feast at New Year banquets. Most foods have symbolic meanings—oranges, dumplings, and a whole fish mean wealth, and eating them brings prosperity into the New Year. To scare away evil spirits, firecrackers are lit and lions are given offerings (usually lucky red envelopes of money) to dance. The bad spirits are also frightened by the bright lanterns, which light the way for the New Year.

And no New Year is complete without the appearance of the lucky dragon. When a new dragon is used for a parade, it can be "woken up" by an eye opening ceremony. This simple ceremony paints in the eyes of the dragon so he can see the symbolic sun (the round shape carried by the parade leader). The dragon chases the sun around and around, ensuring that we will have many nights and days. His chase is accompanied by many merrymakers, whose joyous noise helps scare any remaining evil spirits, guaranteeing a happy, lucky New Year!

good luck sign

bunny lantern

red envelope

drum

dumplings

symbolic sun

qi pao

oranges

noisemaker